MW01252526

Swoon
I'll Catch You
Romantic Lines from the Movies

Ken Bresler

For Sara

I have waited so long for you.

"You don't want to be in love,
you want to be in love in a movie."

Sleepless in Seattle (1993)

*Becky (played by Rosie O'Donnell) speaking to
Annie Reed (played by Meg Ryan).*

*Screenplay by Nora Ephron,
David S. Ward, and Jeff Arch.*

Introduction

Our ambivalence about movie romance—we recognize that it is not real but some of us yearn for movie-style romance anyway—is epitomized by a scene in *Sleepless in Seattle*. In that 1993 movie, the characters Annie Reed (played by Meg Ryan) and Becky (whose last name we don't learn, played by Rosie O'Donnell) watch *An Affair to Remember* in Annie's living room. (That 1957 movie starred Gary Grant and Deborah Kerr.)

Annie: Those were the days when people knew how to be in love.
Becky: You're a basket case.
Annie: They knew it! Time, distance—nothing could separate them because they knew. It was right, it was real, it was—
Becky: A movie. That's your problem. You don't want to be in love, you want to be in love in a movie.

While that scene in the movie belittles movie-style romance—one character calls her friend a basket case with a problem—the entire movie celebrates and encourages us to believe in movie-style romance.

I believe, not necessarily in the *reality* of cinematic

romance, but in the *beauty* of cinematic romance's *lines*. (Well, they're not all lines, despite the subtitle of this collection. This collection contains some dialogues and one long speech.) Some sentiments about love expressed in movies are so breathtakingly and heartachingly beautiful that they resemble a poem by Rumi. Some sentiments amount to wisdom.

For cinema lovers, here are cinematic lovers speaking words of love.

"You should be kissed, and often, and by someone who knows how."

Gone With the Wind (1939)

Rhett Butler (played by Clark Gable) speaking to Scarlett O'Hara (played by Vivien Leigh).

Sidney Howard wrote the screenplay, based on the novel by Margaret Mitchell. The following writers contributed to the screenplay but are uncredited: Oliver H. P. Garrett, Ben Hecht, Jo Swerling, and John Van Druten.

"That thing, that moment, when you kiss someone and everything around you becomes hazy and the only thing in focus is you and this person and you realize that that person is the only person that you're supposed to kiss for the rest of your life, and for one moment you get this amazing gift and you want to laugh and you want to cry because you feel so lucky that you found it and so scared that it will go away, all at the same time."

Never Been Kissed (1999)

Josie Geller (played by Drew Barrymore) to Cynthia (played by Octavia Spencer) and Anita (played by Molly Shannon).

Screenplay by Abby Kohn and Marc Silverstein.

"I was born to kiss you."

Only You (1994)

Faith Corvatch (played by Marisa Tomei) speaking to Peter Wright (played by Robert Downey, Jr.).

Screenplay by Diane Drake.

" We should be lovers,
and that's a fact. "

Moulin Rouge! (2001)

Christian (played by Ewan McGregor) singing to Satine (played by Nicole Kidman).

Baz Luhrmann and Craig Pearce wrote the screenplay, although it is unclear who wrote this lyric in what is called "The Elephant Love Medley."

" . . . I'm scared of walking out of this room and never feeling the rest of my whole life the way I feel when I'm with you. "

Dirty Dancing (1987)

Baby Houseman (played by Jennifer Grey) speaking to Johnny Castle (played by Patrick Swayze).

Eleanor Bergstein wrote the screenplay.

" . . . I think I'd miss you even if we never met. "

Wedding Date (2005)

Nick Mercer (played by Dermot Mulroney) speaking to Kat Ellis (played by Debra Messing).

Dana Fox wrote the screenplay, based on the book by Elizabeth Young.

" You meet thousands of people and none of them really touch you.
And then you meet one person and your life is changed.
Forever. "

Love & Other Drugs (2010)

Jamie Randall (played by Jake Gyllenhaal) speaking to Maggie Murdock (played by Anne Hathaway).

Charles Randolph, Edward Zwick, and Marshall Herskovitz wrote the screenplay, based on the memoir by Jamie Reidy.

These are the last spoken words of the movie.

"If this a crush, I don't think I could take it if the real thing ever happened."

Chasing Amy (1997)

Holden McNeil (played by Ben Affleck) speaking to Alyssa Jones (played by Joey Lauren Adams).

Kevin Smith wrote the screenplay.

"If it wasn't love, it was a lot like it."

A Lot Like Love (2005)

Oliver Martin (played by Ashton Kutcher) speaking to Emily Friehl (played by Amanda Peet).

Screenplay by Colin Patrick Lynch.

"Honestly, if you're not willing to sound stupid, you don't deserve to be in love."

A Lot Like Love (2005)

Emily Friehl (played by Amanda Peet) speaking to Oliver Martin (played by Ashton Kutcher).

Screenplay by Colin Patrick Lynch. This quotation is part of the dialogue that includes the previous quotation.

"I love you. I didn't come here to tell you that I can't live without you. I can live without you. I just don't want to."

Rumor Has It (2005)

Sarah Huttinger (played by Jennifer Aniston) speaking to Jeff Daly (played by Mark Ruffalo).

Screenplay by Ted Griffin.

". . . I love that you are the last person I want to talk to before I go to sleep at night. . . . I came here tonight because when you realize you want to spend the rest of your life with somebody, you want the rest of your life to start as soon as possible.**"**

When Harry Met Sally (1989)

Harry Burns (played by Billy Crystal) speaking to Sally Albright (played by Meg Ryan).

Nora Ephron wrote the screenplay.

"And we are going to last. And you know how I know? Because I still wake up every morning and the first thing I want to do is see your face."

P.S. I Love You (2007)

Gerry Kennedy (played by Gerard Butler) speaking to Holly Kennedy (played by Hilary Swank).

Richard LaGravenese and Steven Rogers wrote the screenplay, based on the novel by Cecelia Ahern.

"I need to know that it's possible that two people can stay happy together forever."

Juno (2007)

Juno MacGuff (played by Ellen Page) speaking to Mac MacGuff (played by J. K. Simmons).

Screenplay by Diablo Cody.

"So it's not going to be easy. It's going to be really hard. And we're going to have to work at this every day, but I want to do that because I want you. I want all of you, forever. You and me. Every day."

The Notebook (2004)

Noah Calhoun (played by Ryan Gosling) speaking to Allie Hamilton (played by Rachel McAdams).

Jeremy Leven wrote the screenplay, which Jan Sardi adapted, based on the novel by Nicholas Sparks.

"Look, I guarantee there'll be tough times. I guarantee that at some point, one or both of us is going want to get out of this thing. But I also guarantee that if I don't ask you to be mine, I'll regret it for the rest of my life, because I know, in my heart, you're the only one for me."

Runaway Bride (1999)

Ike Graham (played by Richard Gere) speaking to Maggie Carpenter (played by Julia Roberts).

"I guarantee that we'll have tough times and I guarantee that at some point, one or both of us will want to get out. But I also guarantee that if I don't ask you to be mine, I'll regret it for the rest of my life, 'cause I know, in my heart, you're the only one for me."

Runaway Bride (1999)

Maggie speaking to Ike.

The two quotations are similar but not identical. The first quotation occurred when Ike suggested to Maggie what a model marriage proposal would sound like. Later, Maggie used his words to affirm that they would get married.

Josann McGibbon and Sara Parriott wrote the screenplay.

"When you fall in love, it is a temporary madness. It erupts like an earthquake, and then it subsides. And when it subsides, you have to make a decision. You have to work out whether your roots have become so entwined together that it is inconceivable that you should ever part. Because this is what love is. Love is not breathlessness, it is not excitement, it is not the desire to mate every second of the day. It is not lying awake at night imagining that he is kissing every part of your body.

No. Don't blush. I am telling you some truths. For that is just being in love, which any of us can convince ourselves we are. Love itself is what is left over, when being in love has burned away. Doesn't sound very exciting, does it? But it is."

Captain Corelli's Mandolin (2001)

Dr. Iannis (played by John Hurt) speaking to Pelagia (played by Penélope Cruz).

Shawn Slovo wrote the screenplay, based on the novel by Louis de Bernières.

" . . . we need a witness to our lives. There's a billion people on the planet. I mean, what does any one life really mean? But in a marriage, you're promising to care about everything. The good things, the bad things, the terrible things, the mundane things. All of it, all of the time, every day. You're saying, 'Your life will not go unnoticed because I will notice it. Your life will not go unwitnessed because I will be your witness.' "

Shall We Dance (2004)

Beverly Clark (played by Susan Sarandon) speaking to Devine (played by Richard Jenkins).

Audrey Wells wrote the screenplay, based on an earlier screenplay by Masayuki Suo.

" I'm . . . just a girl, standing in front of a boy, asking him to love her. "

Notting Hill (1999)

Anna Scott (played by Julia Roberts) speaking to William Thacker (played by Hugh Grant).

Richard Curtis wrote the screenplay.

" Swoon. I'll catch you. "

The English Patient (1996)

*Almásy (played by Ralph Fiennes) speaking to
Katharine Clifton (played by Kristin Scott Thomas).*

*Anthony Minghella wrote the screenplay, based on
the novel by Michael Ondaatje.*

"All my words. And every heartbeat. They're all for you."

The Edge of Love (2008)

Dylan Thomas (played by Matthew Rhys) speaking to Caitlin Thomas (played by Sienna Miller).

Screenplay by Sharman Macdonald and Rebekah Gilbertson.

"First love is all right, as far as it goes. Last love—that's what I'm interested in."

The Edge of Love (2008)

William Killick (played by Cillian Murphy) speaking to Vera Phillips (played by Keira Knightley).

Screenplay by Sharman Macdonald and Rebekah Gilbertson.

" There is a place you can touch a woman that will drive her crazy. . . . Her heart. "

Milk Money (1994)

V (played by Melanie Griffith) speaking to Frank (played by Michael Patrick Carter), Tom (played by Ed Harris), Kevin (played by Brian Christopher), and Brad (played by Adam LaVorgna).

Screenplay by John Mattson.

> **❝ . . . love denied blights the soul we owe to God. ❞**

Shakespeare in Love (1998)

Will Shakespeare (played by Joseph Fiennes) speaking to Viola de Lesseps, disguised as Thomas Kent (played by Gwyneth Paltrow).

Screenplay by Marc Norman and Tom Stoppard.

" I have crossed oceans of time to find you. "

Bram Stoker's Dracula (1992)

Dracula (played by Gary Oldman) speaking to Mina Murray (played by Winona Ryder).

James V. Hart wrote the screenplay, based on the novel by Bram Stoker.

" It seems right now that all I've ever done in my life is making my way here to you. "

Bridges of Madison County (1995)

Robert Kincaid (played by Clint Eastwood) speaking to Francesca Johnson (played by Meryl Streep).

Richard LaGravenese wrote the screenplay, based on the novel by Robert James.

"Don't say we're not right for each other because the way I see it we might not be right for anybody else. . . . It can't be any harder to stay together than it was to stay apart."

The Cutting Edge (1992)

Doug Dorsey (played by D. B. Sweeney) speaking to Kate (played by Moira Kelly).

Tony Gilroy wrote the screenplay.

"I'd rather fight with you than make love with anyone else."

Wedding Date (2005)

Nick Mercer (played by Dermot Mulroney) speaking to Kat Ellis (played by Debra Messing).

Dana Fox wrote the screenplay, based on the book by Elizabeth Young.

"You're not perfect, sport, and let me save you the suspense: This girl you've met, she isn't perfect either. But the question is whether or not you're perfect for each other."

Good Will Hunting (1997)

Sean Maguire (played by Robin Williams) speaking to Will Hunting (played by Matt Damon).

Matt Damon and Ben Affleck wrote the screenplay.

“ . . . love is friendship on fire.**”**

The Perfect Man (2005)

Adam Forrest (played by Ben Feldman) emailing Holly Hamilton (played by Hilary Duff).

Gina Wendkos wrote the screenplay.

" If you're going to marry someone, it might as well be your best friend. "

Rumor Has It (2005)

Sarah Huttinger (played by Jennifer Aniston) speaking to Annie Huttinger (played by Mena Suvari).

Screenplay by Ted Griffin.

"I love you. And not, not in a friendly way, although I think we're great friends. And not in a misplaced-affection, puppy-dog way, although I'm sure that's what you'll call it. I love you. Very, very simple, very truly. You are the epitome of everything I have ever looked for in another human being. And I know that you think of me as just a friend, and crossing that line is the furthest thing from an option you would ever consider. But I had to say it. I just, I can't take this anymore. I can't stand next to you without wanting to hold you. I can't look into your eyes without feeling that longing you only read about in trashy romance novels. I can't talk to

you without wanting to express
my love for everything you are.
And I know this will probably
queer our friendship, no pun
intended, but I had to say it,
'cause I've never felt this way
before, and I don't care. I like
who I am because of it. And if
bringing this to light means we
can't hang out anymore, then
that hurts me. But God, I just,
I couldn't allow another day to
go by without just getting it out
there, regardless of the outcome,
which by the look on your face
is to be the inevitable shoot-
down. And, you know, I'll accept
that. But I know, I know that
some part of you is hesitating
for a moment, and if there's a
moment of hesitation, then that

means you feel something too. And all I ask, please, is that you just not dismiss that, and try to dwell in it for just ten seconds. God. Alyssa, there isn't another soul on this f—ing planet who has ever made me half the person I am when I'm with you, and I would risk this friendship for the chance to take it to the next plateau, because it is there between you and me. You can't deny that. Even if, you know, even if we never talk again after tonight, please know that I am forever changed because of who you are and what you've meant to me. . . . ""

Chasing Amy (1997)

Holden McNeil (played by Ben Affleck) speaking to Alyssa Jones (played by Joey Lauren Adams).

Kevin Smith wrote the screenplay.

"You turned out to be all that I was looking for. The missing piece in the big f—ing puzzle. "

Chasing Amy (1997)

Alyssa Jones (played by Joey Lauren Adams) speaking to Holden McNeil (played by Ben Affleck).

Kevin Smith wrote the screenplay.

Jerry Maguire: Hello?
Hello. I'm looking for my wife.
… I love you. You complete
me. And I just had–
Dorothy Boyd: Shut up.
Just shut up. You had me at
'Hello.' You had me at 'Hello.'

Jerry Maguire (1996)

*Tom Cruise played Jerry Maguire. Renée Zellweger
played Dorothy Boyd.*

Screenplay by Cameron Crowe.

*"You had me at 'Hello'" is the most frequently cited
romantic line from* Jerry Maguire *on the internet.
"You complete me" is the second most frequently
cited romantic line. The lines are related and so they
are presented together here.*

*"You had me at 'Hello'" is not about love at first
sight or love at first greeting, despite a recurring
misconception on the internet and off. The two romantic
leads were married, and Dorothy was referring to
Jerry's hellos to a living room full of women.*

"You are everything I never knew I always wanted."

Fools Rush In (1997)

Alex Whitman (played by Matthew Perry)
speaking to Isabel Fuentes (played by Salma Hayek).

Katherine Reback wrote the screenplay. Joan
Taylor and Katherine Reback wrote the story.

" I am someone else with you,
someone more like myself. "

Original Sin (2001)

Luis Antonio Vargas (played by Antonio Banderas) speaking to Bonny Castle, posing as Julia Russell (played by Angelina Jolie).

Michael Cristofer wrote the screenplay, based on the novel by Cornell Woolrich.

"I'm happiest when I'm being myself, and I'm myself when I'm with you."

What's Your Number? (2011)

Ally Darling (played by Anna Faris) speaking to Colin Shea (played by Chris Evans).

Gabrielle Allan and Jennifer Crittenden wrote the screenplay, based on the novel by Karyn Bosnak.

"Soulmates. It's extremely rare, but it exists. It's sort of like twin souls tuned into each other."

What Dreams May Come (1998)

Albert (played by Cuba Gooding, Jr.) speaking to Chris Nielsen (played by Robin Williams).

Ronald Bass wrote the screenplay, based on the novel by Richard Matheson.

" There are those that do not believe that a single soul born in heaven can split into twin spirits and shoot like falling stars to earth, where over oceans and continents their magnetic forces will finally unite them back into one. But, how else to explain love at first sight? "

Don Juan DeMarco (1994)

Don Juan DeMarco (played by Johnny Depp) speaking to Dr. Jack Mickler (played by Marlon Brando).

Jeremy Leven wrote the screenplay.

"There are only four questions of value in life. . . . What is sacred? Of what is the spirit made? What is worth living for, and what is worth dying for? The answer to each is the same: Only love."

Don Juan DeMarco (1994)

Don Juan DeMarco (played by Johnny Depp) speaking to Dr. Jack Mickler (played by Marlon Brando).

Jeremy Leven wrote the screenplay.

"I love you too much. But I cannot love you any less."

Don Juan DeMarco (1994)

Don Juan DeMarco (played by Johnny Depp) speaking to Doña Ana (played by Géraldine Pailhas).

Jeremy Leven wrote the screenplay.

"Have you never met a woman who inspires you to love? Until your every sense is filled with her? You inhale her. You taste her. You see your unborn children in her eyes and know that your heart has at last found a home. Your life begins with her, and without her, it must surely end."

Don Juan DeMarco (1994)

Don Juan DeMarco (played by Johnny Depp) speaking to Dr. Jack Mickler (played by Marlon Brando).

Jeremy Leven wrote the screenplay.

" . . . God put an angel on earth just for you. Who could rescue you from the depths of hell. "

Good Will Hunting (1997)

Sean Maguire (played by Robin Williams) speaking to Will Hunting (played by Matt Damon).

Matt Damon and Ben Affleck wrote the screenplay.

" I have not slept for fear I would wake to find all this a dream. "

Ever After: A Cinderella Story (1998)

Prince Henry (played by Dougray Scott) speaking to Danielle (played by Drew Barrymore).

Susannah Grant, Andy Tennant, and Rick Parks wrote the screenplay.

" You know that place between sleep and awake? That place where you still remember dreaming? That's where I'll always love you. . . . That's where I'll be waiting. "

Hook (1991)

Tinkerbell (played by Julia Roberts) speaking to Peter Banning (played by Robin Williams).

Jim V. Hart and Malia Scotch Marmo wrote the screenplay, and Hart and Nick Castle wrote the screen story, based on the books and play by J. M. Barrie.

"If I could ask God one thing, it would be to stop the moon. Stop the moon and make this night and your beauty last forever."

A Knight's Tale (2001)

William Thatcher (played by Heath Ledger) speaking to Jocelyn (played by Shannyn Sossamon).

Brian Helgeland wrote the screenplay.

"No measure of time with you will be long enough. But let's start with forever."

The Twilight Saga: Breaking Dawn - Part 1 (2011)

Edward Cullen (played by Robert Pattinson) speaking to Bella Swan (played by Kristen Stewart).

Melissa Rosenberg wrote the screenplay, based on the novel by Stephenie Meyer.

" I'd rather die tomorrow than live a hundred years without knowing you. "

Pocahontas (1995)

John Smith (voiced by Mel Gibson) speaking to Pocahantas (voiced by Irene Bedard).

Carl Binder, Susannah Grant, and Philip LaZebnik wrote the screenplay, with numerous other people sharing credits.

" I would rather share one lifetime with you than face all the ages of this world alone. "

The Lord of the Rings: The Fellowship of the Ring (2001)

Arwen (played by Liv Tyler) speaking to Aragorn (played by Viggo Mortensen).

Fran Walsh, Philippa Boyens, and Peter Jackson wrote the screenplay, based on the novel by J. R. R. Tolkien.

Li Mu Bai: Shu Lien.

Lu Shu Lien: Shh. Save your strength.

Mu Bai: My life is departing. I've only one breath left.

Shu Lien: Use it to meditate. Free yourself from this world, as you have been taught. Let your soul rise to eternity with your last breath. Do not waste it for me.

Mu Bai: I've already wasted my whole life. I want to tell you with my last breath that I have always loved you. I would rather be a ghost drifting by your side as a condemned soul than enter heaven without you. Because of your love, I will never be a lonely spirit.

Crouching Tiger, Hidden Dragon (2000)

Yun-Fat Chow played Li Mu Bai. Michelle Yeow played Lu Shu Lien.

Hui-Ling Wang, James Schamus, and Kuo Jung Tsai wrote the screenplay, based on the book by Du Lu Wang

These are the subtitles; the movie was performed in Mandarin. These are not quotations from the English dubbed versions.

I would rather have had one breath of her hair, one kiss of her mouth, one touch of her hand, than an eternity without it. One.

City of Angels (1998)

Seth (played by Nicholas Cage) speaking to Cassiel (played by Andre Braugher).

Wim Wenders, Peter Handke, Richard Reitinger, and Dana Stevens wrote the screenplay.

These are the last spoken words of the movie.

Afterword

Although a common belief about movie-style romance is that it is not realistic, at least four of the quotations in this collection involve the practicalities of love, romance, and marriage: *The Notebook*, p. 25; *Runaway Bride*, pp. 26-27; *Captain Corelli's Mandolin*, pp. 28-29; and *Shall We Dance*, p. 30. The last quotation specifically invokes "the bad things, the terrible things, the mundane things. All of it, all of the time, every day."

Characters in four movies discounted the love lines in this collection, perhaps reflecting the writers' self-consciousness that they had crafted striking sentiments. When Maggie spoke Ike's words back to him in *Runaway Bride* (p.27), he responded, "That's a pretty good speech, Maggie."

In *The Edge of Love*, after William spoke to Vera of first and last love (p. 34), she dismissed him by saying, "Oh, you think you're so damned wise."

In *Fools Rush In*, Alex said to Isabel, "You are everything I never knew I always wanted" (p. 49), and then added, "I'm not even sure what that means exactly . . . ."

And in *Shall We Dance*, Beverly pronounced that "we need a witness to our lives" (p. 30). When she's done explaining what she means, she continues, "You can quote me on that if you like."

Well, yes, I would like to quote you, and I do.

You may have noticed some themes in these quotations. Here are some:

Shoulds

I would rather

Who I Am With You

The rest of my life

Forever and always

God's role

Finally, you may have noticed that Julia Roberts delivered three quotations in this collection: *Runaway Bride*, p. 27; *Notting Hill*, p. 31; and *Hook*, p. 59.

Collecting the Quotations

I verified these quotations by watching the movies and writing down the quotations—or in the case of the one foreign film, writing down the subtitles. These are the lines and speeches as spoken, not as written; I didn't examine the screenplays.

This won't surprise you, but the internet inaccurately cites many purported quotations. The line from *Good Will Hunting* about perfection appears online in an altered form that seems to have been passed around from web page to web page without anyone verifying it. Wonderfully romantic lines that various internet sites attribute to four movies are not actually uttered in those movies, much to my disappointment.

I listened hard. One purported quotation from *City of Angels* is rendered online as "I would rather have had . . . one kiss from her mouth . . . than eternity without it." (I have excerpted the larger quotation here.) But no, that's not it. The words are "one kiss *of* her mouth" and "*an* eternity."

Punctuating the spoken word is an inexact art. I may have heard a period, whereas someone else heard a comma. Someone else may have heard a comma and I heard a dash. The most famous love line from *Jerry Maguire* is almost always rendered as "You had me at hello." But isn't it really "You had me at 'Hello'"? That's how I've rendered it here.

Many of these lines come toward the end of the movies, as if the entire movie led up to a grandly romantic pronouncement. Examples include *Runaway Bride*, *Milk Money*, and *Crouching Tiger, Hidden Dragon*. The quotations from *Love & Other Drugs* and *City of Angels* in this collection entail the last spoken words of the two movies. One exception is *Never Been Kissed*, where the quotation about a kiss comes toward the beginning of the movie, setting up the movie.

In general, I glossed over the context of these quotations, leaving it to readers of this collection to supply the context, by being familiar with the movies or viewing them. Two exceptions are R*unaway Bride*, p.27, and *Jerry Maguire*, p. 48, for which I supplied explanatory notes.

I don't consider infidelity to be romantic. I included lines involving unfaithful lovers and spouses only after some thought and hesitation.

Just because I've included a quotation doesn't mean that I subscribe to it. For example, *The Cutting Edge* includes this line: "It can't be any harder to stay together than it was to stay apart." I don't believe that's enough of a reason for a couple to stay together. While some of the quotations in this collection entail one character advising another, be careful of taking any of these quotations as advice.

Favorites

Alone or with your friend, lover, or spouse, discuss which quotations are your favorites. Why? Because of their beauty? Because of their truth? Because you have felt that way?

Write Your Own

I once read about a recording artist who considered an album to be the soundtrack for a movie that hadn't been made yet. Sit down alone or with your friend, lover, or spouse. Create lines from movies that haven't been made yet or lines from imaginary movies. For example: "I get lost in your blue eyes. I want to swim in them."

Here are mine:

"You are on time, my dear. Still, I have been waiting so long for you."

"Galileo was wrong and so was the Church. The universe doesn't revolve around the sun or the earth. It revolves around my heart and my love for you."

"I trick myself into thinking that
it was all a dream, you and me,
a lovely dream about things that
vanished when I woke up, lovely
things that weren't mine to keep.
Because if I thought they were
memories, and once I could
touch and kiss and keep you, my
heart couldn't keep on beating."

Credits

I don't know movies well enough to have compiled this list on my own. Numerous blogs and websites pointed me toward quotations that I was not familiar with and movies I had not heard of.

The Newton Free Library, Newton, Massachusetts, located the movies that I watched to verify the quotations.

IMDB.com, the internet movie database, provided me with vital information about the movies, including their screenwriters.

Deborah Fogel and Judah Levine generously contributed their editorial skills once again. I am grateful.

And once again, Doreen Hann performed her book design magic.

The Editor

Ken Bresler is a writer and occasional poet in Newton, Massachusetts. He compiled and edited *Mark Twain vs. Lawyers, Lawmakers, and Lawbreakers: Humorous Observations*; and *Can You Dance A Prayer?: Collected Wisdom About Praying*. He wrote *Poetry Made Visible: Boston Sites for Poetry Lovers, Art Lovers & Lovers*; and *H. H. Richardson: Three Architectural Tours*.

Made in the USA
Middletown, DE
09 July 2021

43621129R00046